This book belongs to

....

Waltham Forest Libraries	
904 000 00650523	
Askews & Holts	19-Jul-2019
FIR	£4.99
6085578	

© 2019 Quarto Publishing plc

First published in 2019 by QED Publishing, an imprint of The Quarto Group. The Old Brewery, 6 Blundell Street, London N7 9BH, United Kingdom. T (0)20 7700 6700 F (0)20 7700 8066 www.QuartoKnows.com

A catalogue record for this book is available from the British Library.

ISBN 978-0-71124-383-5

Based on the original story by Peter Bently and Duncan Beedie

Author of adapted text: Katie Woolley
Series Editor: Joyce Bentley
Series Designer: Sarah Peden

Manufactured in Shenzhen, China PP052019

9 8 7 6 5 4 3 2 1

MIX
Paper from responsible sources
FSC® C001701

Reading
Gems

Pem's Little Brother

QED

Focus sounds in this book

ear
hear

air
air

ure
manure

igh
night

a-e
cave

e-e
these

i-e
slice

o-e
woke

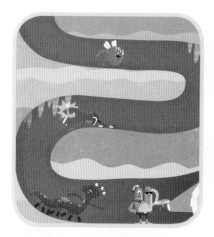

u-e
huge

zh
treasure

Ready?
Let's Go!

5

The bugs.

I am Nid.

I am San.

I am Gop.

I am Pem.

"I can hear a noise," said Nid.

A ship was high up in the air.

"It's Huff, my little brother," said Pem.

"I have come here to visit from Planet Nip," said Huff.

First Huff did not like Pem's cake.

"It is like manure!" he said.

So Pem got him some ripe fruit.

Then the bugs went out to the fair.

"Come on," said Huff. "We can race there!"

Huff slept in Pem's bed.

He kept Pem awake at night.

When Huff woke up, he ate Pem's food. "These little ones are yum!" he said.

But Huff did not like
the moon stones.

"I do not like Planet Bug!"

What a rude bug Huff was!

Just then, Huff found a cave.

"There might be treasure in here!"
he said.

The cave was huge!

The bugs came to a green stone.

The stone was stuck tight!

So Huff ran at it with all his might.

Pop! Huff fell straight into the lake!

It was hard to get him out!

"It is time for me to go," said Huff.
He zoomed high into the air.

"Nid, you were the stone!" said Gop.

"You got rid of Huff!"

All the bugs were glad.

They had a slice of Pem's cake.

Let's Talk About Pem's Little Brother

Look at the back cover.

Point to the focus letters.

Can you make the letter sounds?

Can you find the tricky words in the story?

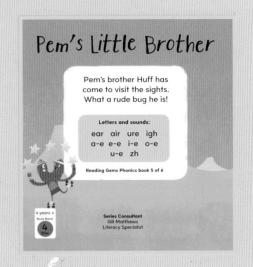

Pem's Little Brother

Pem's brother Huff has come to visit the sights. What a rude bug he is!

Letters and sounds:
ear air ure igh
a-e e-e i-e o-e
u-e zh

Reading Gems Phonics book 5 of 6

4 years +
Book Band
4
Blue

Series Consultant
Gill Matthews
Literacy Specialist

Find the letters 'igh' in the word 'night' on page 12.

What sound does 'igh' make?

Can you find some other words in the story with the letters 'igh' in them?

Can you think of any other words with 'igh' in them?

This story looks at split digraphs such as a-e in 'ate'.

Can you sound out these split digraphs?

e-e   i-e   o-e   u-e

Can you find them in the story?

Why did the bugs not like Huff?

How did Huff behave during his visit?

What did the bugs do at the end of the story?

Did you like the story about Pem's little brother?

What was your favourite bit?

27

Fun and Games

Look at the letters in the box.
Use them to complete the words below.

| igh | ear | e-e | i-e | ure | a-e |

n_____t

c____k____

h_____

r__p__

th__s__

man_____

The bugs are lost in the cave.
Can you unjumble the tricky words and
follow the tunnel to help them get out?

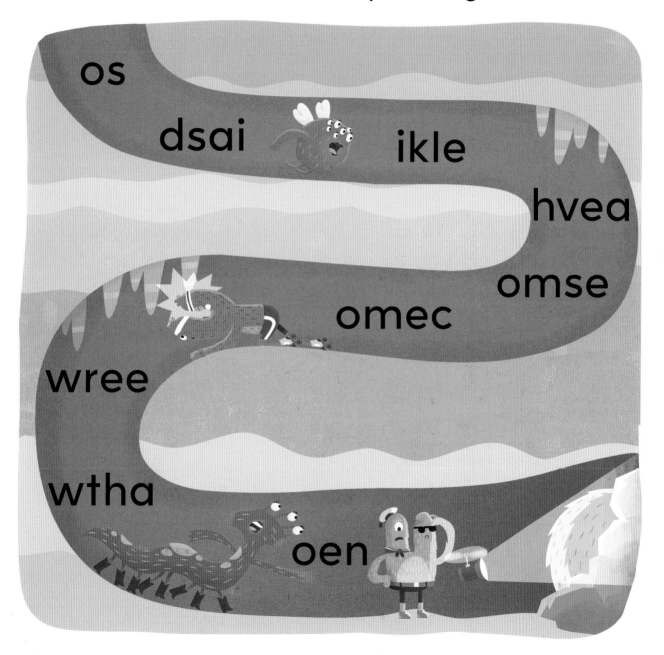

os

dsai

ikle

hvea

omse

omec

wree

wtha

oen

Answers: so; said; like; have; some; come; were; what and one.

Reading With Your Little Bugs

Here are some tips to help you enjoy reading this book with your child.

1 Encourage your child to read the story to you, saying the sounds and putting them together to read the word.

2 If your child gets stuck on a word, show them how to break it down into sounds.

3 Have fun! You could make up silly voices for each of the characters and even act out the story together.

4 Remember to give your child lots of praise!

5 If your child is starting to feel tired or bored, put the book away and pick it up another day.

Have fun and enjoy reading my story together.

Mind-Boggling Phonics Glossary

Phonics often feels a bit confusing,
with lots of alien terms. This glossary
will help demystify Phonics!

blend to put individual sounds together to read a word, e.g. s-n-a-p blended together reads 'snap'.

CVC word a word spelled with a consonant, then a vowel, then a consonant, like 'sat' or 'tip'.

decode to put sounds and letters together to read a word correctly.

digraph two letters representing one sound, e.g. ck in 'kick'.

grapheme a letter or group of letters representing one sound, e.g. t, b, sh, ch, igh, ough (as in 'though').

phoneme a single unit of sound, e.g. the letter 't' represents just one sound and the letters 'sh' represent just one sound.

segment to split up a word into its individual phonemes in order to spell, e.g. the word 'cat' has three phonemes: /c/ /a/ /t/.

sight words or high-frequency words are words that appear most often in printed materials. They may not be decodable using phonics (or too advanced) but they are useful to learn separately by sight to develop fluency in reading.

tricky words are words that cannot be sounded out with phonics, such as 'the', 'was' and 'one'. Sometimes called exception words.

trigraph three letters representing one sound, e.g. igh in 'night'.

GET TO KNOW READING GEMS

Reading Gems is a series of books that has been written for children who are learning to read. The books have been created in consultation with a literacy specialist.

The books fit into five levels, with each level getting more challenging as a child's confidence and reading ability grows. The simple text and fun illustrations provide gradual, structured practice of reading. Most importantly, these books are good stories that are fun to read!

Phonics is for children who are learning their letters and sounds. Simple, engaging stories provide gentle phonics practice.

Level 1 is for children who are taking their first steps into reading. Story themes and subjects are familiar to young children, and there is lots of repetition to build reading confidence.

Level 2 is for children who have taken their first reading steps and are becoming readers. Story themes are still familiar but sentences are a bit longer, as children begin to tackle more challenging vocabulary.

Level 3 is for children who are developing as readers. Stories and subjects are varied, and more descriptive words are introduced.

Level 4 is for readers who are rapidly growing in reading confidence and independence. There is less repetition on the page, broader themes are explored and plot lines straddle multiple pages.

Phonics